FOR CHRIS - BEARD MUSE.
OH, AND ALSO FOR MY MUM
BECAUSE I WANT THIS WAR TO END.

OXFORD
UNIVERSITY PRESS

Great Clarendon Street, Oxford OX2 6DP

Oxford University Press is a department of the University of Oxford.
It furthers the University's objective of excellence in research, scholarship, and
education by publishing worldwide. Oxford is a registered trade mark of Oxford
University Press in the UK and in certain other countries

First published 2018

British Library Cataloguing in Publication Data

Data available

ISBN: 978-0-19-276396-9

1 3 5 7 9 10 8 6 4 2

Printed in Great Britain

Paper used in the production of this book is a natural,
recyclable product made from wood grown in sustainable forests.
The manufacturing process conforms to the environmental
regulations of the country of origin.

WIZARDING FOR BEGINNERS

FROM THE
MOST BONKERS MIND OF

ELYS DOLAN

OXFORD
UNIVERSITY PRESS

Chapter 1

There was once a dragon. A dragon called Dave. Not only was Dave a dragon, he was also a brave and fearless knight. Aided by his trusty steed, a goat named Albrecht, Dave performed the most heroic of deeds. He defeated villains, saved entire kingdoms, and awoke sleeping princesses . . .

. . . but there was none of that happening right now because today it was a Tuesday and that's when Dave had his book club.

Dave and Albrecht had been living happily in Castletown ever since Dave got his knighthood and Albrecht had agreed to stay on as Dave's trusty steed and life coach. They were even getting involved with the local community, hence the book club. Dave had been looking forward to discussing the new romance novel they'd been reading but Albrecht just wouldn't keep quiet.

... and you can see I still have the muscles from my competition days ...

'Albrecht!' said Dave. 'You know usually I'd be happy to listen to your stories but right now we're trying to . . .'

Dave was interrupted by the post coming through the door.

'Wunderbar!' yelled Albrecht as he picked up the letters. 'I have ordered some new fur cream to get the best shine and my subscription to *Outlandish Adventurers* is due today. It's the issue where they interviewed me about my new steed work and there is a picture of me . . .'

Albrecht suddenly went quiet which was not a very Albrecht thing to do.

Dave tottered over to see if everything was all right.

'Mein Dave,' said Albrecht.
'Look! They have sent
another one.'

Albrecht flipped the
postcard over.

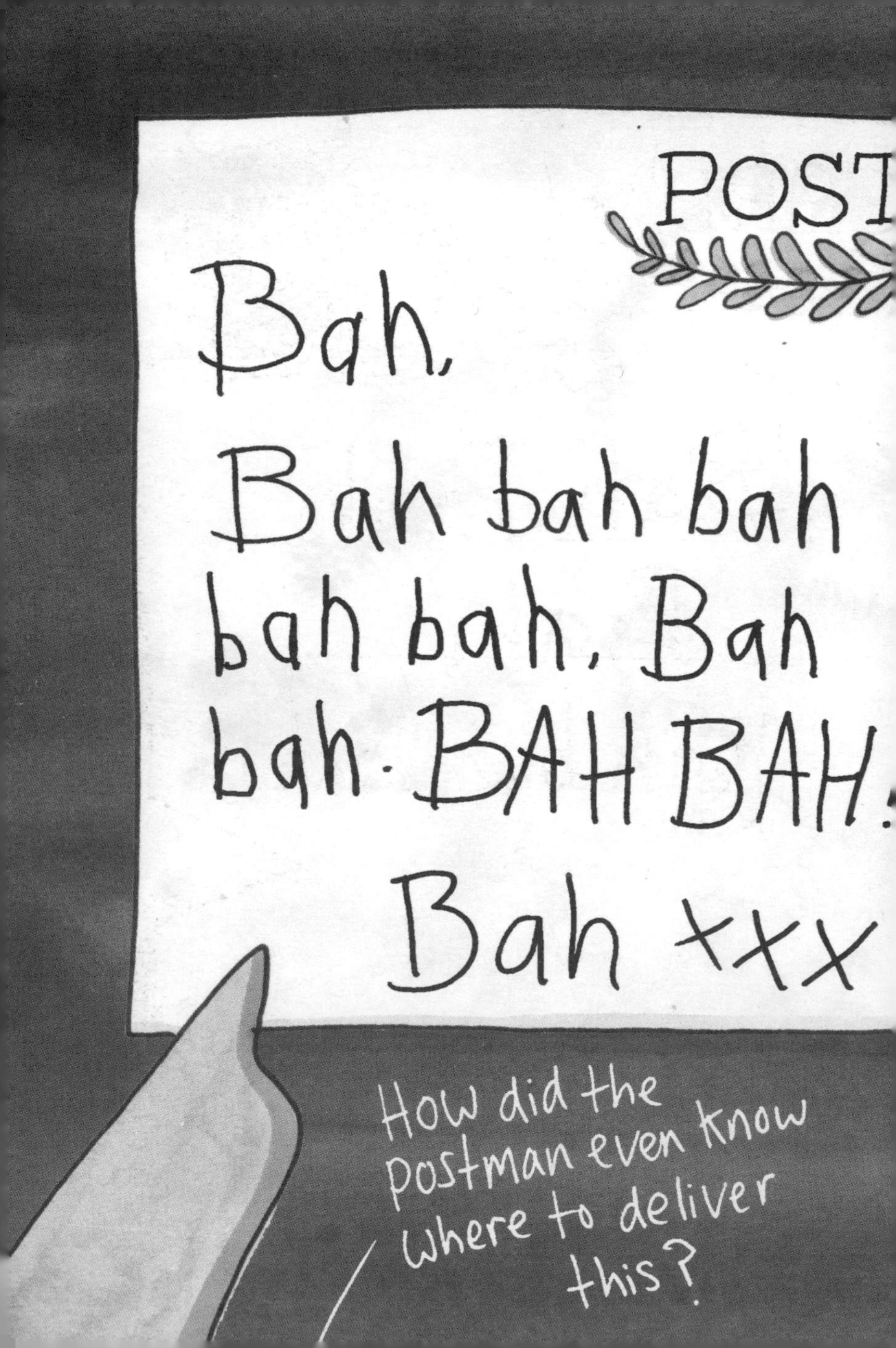
POST
Bah,
Bah bah bah bah bah, Bah bah. BAH BAH
Bah xxx
How did the postman even know where to deliver this?

'Dumme goats!' said Albrecht. 'Do they not
know I cannot understand them!'

The rest of the book club, consisting of Mildred the Bearded Lady and Boil Man (he has boils), came over to see what the commotion was about.

'Who can't you understand?' said Mildred.

'It is my family,' said Albrecht. 'All they can say is "bah, bah, bah". I think they are trying to invite me to weddings and send the Christmas cards but I just do not know. When I was a kid I was just one of the herd, until that wizard cast a spell on me and made me talk. It was a curse with mixed blessings—I have the gift of speech but can no longer converse with those who know me best—my own kin! I am a great adventurer, steed and life coach, but I can no longer understand my own family and it is clear that they no longer understand me. It is my greatest regret that I cannot tell them all of my super amazing stories.'

'I really think you should just go and see them,' said Dave. 'You'll probably have loads in common, like making lots of noise and eating everything, even if you don't speak Goat.'

'Pah—I am no longer one of the herd. My life is too different now. I don't want to talk about it anymore—thinking of that Wizard, Terrence the

Terrible is bringing back bad memories!' Albrecht sniffed.

'Are you OK?' asked Dave.

'Of course I'm OK! Nothing fazes a professional adventure-goat like me! Now let's all look at the picture of me in *Outlandish Adventurer*...'

'Albrecht, you're avoiding the subject,' said Mildred. 'You should really talk about this with someone. You're not the only animal Terrence the Terrible made talk. HRH Gilbert the Frog has started a Talking Animal Support Group. It's just about to start up at the castle so get out of here and then we can actually get on with our book club.'

Fine! But only because someone might finally look at my photos.

OUTLANDISH ADVENTURER ALBRECHT

STEED?

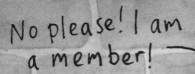

CHAPTER 2

Over at the castle Albrecht joined in the Talking
Animal Support Group. It was a safe space where
talking animals could discuss their feelings about
the terrible Wizard who made them this way.
Also, there were donuts.

It was actually a pretty good meeting. HRH Gilbert the frog, married to Princess Rubella, let them use the castle hall because Rubella and the King were away on their annual father daughter fishing trip. Everyone was friendly and there were even the donuts with sprinkles that Albrecht likes. Plus, he was learning so much more about the Wizard, Terrence . . .

He Said his name was Terrence the Terrible!

Why did he even want us to talk?

He got me to brush my hair and Say some magic words but it just made him angry.

Now that I can talk. everyone just assumes that I want to chat.

Finally, it was Albrecht's turn.

'We have a new member of our support group,' said Gilbert. 'This is Albrecht. Say hello everyone.'

'Hello Albrecht,' all the animals said together.

Albrecht stood up. 'Guten Tag! I am Albrecht and I am a talking animal. I would like to tell you about my picture in *Outlandish Adventurer.*'

'Actually Albrecht,' interrupted Gilbert, 'do you think you could talk about the Wizard first?'

'Well there was a frog and a potion and then I could talk!

'I escaped and ran back to my family but they couldn't understand me, so I had to leave. It was then that I realized that the only goat I could rely on was me.'

Albrecht was interrupted by the door banging open and some uninvited guests striding in.

Good afternoon. I am Reginald Fox Esq. attorney-at-law. This is my personal assistant Andrew and this huge tiger is Barry and if you don't do exactly as I say, Barry will definitely eat you.

I'm here to deliver a summons.
My client, the wizard who made
you all talk, asserts that he
bought/stole/kidnapped you
fair and square. I shall escort
you back to the Guild of
Wizards immediately and
you'd best cooperate because
Barry is
Peckish.

Fellow talking animals, I will save you!

CHAPTER 3

'Fear not fellow talking animals, Albrecht will single-handedly save the day!' Albrecht leapt out of his seat, ready for battle.

Albrecht sped through Castletown to get home and find Dave. He hadn't run like this since his time in the Olympics! He'd got a silver medal with only a little cheating.

Give that back!

Albrecht flung himself through the door and Dave looked alarmed. 'Albrecht! Are you OK? You're sweatier than usual.'

'Tiger . . . wizard . . . fox assistant . . . donut attack . . . animals gone!' Once Albrecht caught his breath and started making sense, he explained to the book club what had happened.

'You and Dave will have to go to the Guild of Wizards and rescue those animals!' said Mildred. 'I can't go, I have my Foundlings School for Girls with Moustaches to take care of, and Boil Man is kind of unreliable.'

'The thing with the cart crash, and the spillage, and the escaped sheep, and the forest fire wasn't my fault!' said Boil Man.

'And you are well known around here for being adventurous heroes with no fear of danger,' added Mildred.

'I'm actually not a big fan of danger. I'm more of a moderate risk kind of dragon . . .' said Dave.

Albrecht waved his hooves dramatically. 'I can go alone!'

'No,' said Dave. 'We're a team. I'm coming too.'

'Fine, but only because it will be a good learning experience for you kleiner Dave. We'll need disguises of course,' declared Albrecht.

'Then we'll have to convince the Guild of Wizards that we're wizards too! I have just the thing to help. I was saving this for next month's book club but we might need to read it now.' Dave pulled something off the book shelf.

WIZARDING

✴ FOR ✴

BEGINNERS

SPELLS
SPELLS
SPELLS

GET THE LOOK
WIZARD CHIC

HATS: the taller the hat the more important you look.

'Ooo, you must be important!'

'I respect you as a wizard.'

'Do you make the tea?'

'Who even cares?'

ACCESSORIES

Frogs

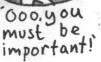

Makes you seem better looking?

SPELL BOOK

Fancy Stick. Not magic, just looks impressive.

BEARDS

All Wizards must have a big, excellent beard to look awesome.

EXTRA LONG

THE PUFFBALL

POINTY

CURLY CURL

NO TO

GOATEES

CHAPTER 4

'If we borrow a couple of beards from Mildred and stick a few stars on our pyjamas those wizards will never know we're not one of them!'

After borrowing a few things from Mildred and from Boil Man's dressing up box, they were ready. The results were surprisingly convincing, if you ignored how green Dave was and the fact that Albrecht was a goat.

Mein Dave, I love this beard.

Will we ever have an adventure where I don't wear fake hair?

'I really think we should practise some magic Albrecht. What if there's a test?' said Dave. 'There are sample spells in the book and we could have a study party on the journey!'

'Pfft! Albrecht has no need of Dummkopf wizard rubbish or boring parties! I shall spend the time re-styling my fabulous beard.'

Typical Albrecht, thought Dave. He flipped open the book and sat down to read as they set out for the Guild of Wizards.

Albrecht, is that my dressing gown?

Auf Wiedersehen.

Oh that's not flowers.

LING

NOT OVER HERE!

CHAPTER 5

'Those wizards must love signs,' said Albrecht as they walked through the gates towards the Guild of Wizards.

'It looks like they have a lot of rules,' said Dave. 'Let me check the book.'

Rules of the Guild of Wizards

- ★ Absolutely <u>NO</u> girls allowed
- ★ Beards compulsory
- ★ Everything stops for meals
- ★ Hats compulsory
- ★ No running. except on Thursdays when running is compulsory
- ★ Luggage must not exceed 55x40x20cm
- ★ No shoes on the carpet unless it's a full moon
- ★ If your name begins with A-M keep off the grass
- ★ If your name begins with N-Z do not leave the grass

'There are another eighty-four pages of these!' said Dave.

'I have no time for other people's rules,' said Albrecht. 'We must get inside and find the animals. I gave them my word. I will scale the walls, shimmy along the roof, lower myself down by rope into an upstairs room and pretend I have been there all along.'

'Or we could ring the doorbell?' said Dave.

They opted for Dave's method. After a few rings the door was opened by a group of elaborately bearded men in pointy hats.

The wizard at the front gave them a suspicious look. 'You're not girls, are you? Girls are most definitely not allowed in here.'

No girls! thought Dave. What rubbish! Dave puffed himself up, ready to give the wizard a piece of his mind when Albrecht stepped in.

'We are dumme wizards just like you! Look at our incredible beards. No girl has these.'

'Try and tell Mildred that,' whispered Dave.

'Shhhh Dave!' Albrecht put a hoof over Dave's mouth. 'We are but two travelling wizards on our way to a beard convention. Maybe you kind

31

brother wizards will give us a bed for the night?'

The wizard looked sceptical. 'What are your names?'

Albrecht made introductions but the wizard wasn't satisfied. 'No, what are your *wizard* names? For instance, I'm The Amazing Arnold, this is Miraculous Mark and that's The Wondrous Clive.' Albrecht knew exactly what his wizard name should be.

'Never heard of you. To prove you're really wizards you must demonstrate your magic! Any trick will do.'

Dave knew it! There's always a test. He'd been practising magicking a bunch of flowers out of his sleeve the whole journey there. Dave assumed the position.

'It's rubbish but I suppose it's magic,' said Arnold. 'Tall one, it's your go!'

Albrecht hadn't practised any magic so Dave didn't think this would go well.

All the wizards broke into applause. 'I have never seen anything so exotic!' said Arnold. 'Have you ever considered doing it at parties?'

Dave was quite annoyed that Albrecht's silly balloon trick had impressed them more than his magic but at least they would be allowed inside now.

Arnold led them into the entrance hall.

'Welcome chaps! Now you must come to dinner. It starts in about 8.2 minutes and Rule 482 does mention that it's compulsory.'

Albrecht rolled his eyes at the mention of rules as Arnold continued. 'And I should mention that we're having just a little bit of a tiger problem at the moment, so sorry about the mess.'

Arnold stopped to fuss over some claw marks in the woodwork as Dave and Albrecht started whispering.

'Albrecht!' said Dave. 'This must be the tiger that helped kidnap the other animals!'

'Ja, which means we must be in the right place! Let's go and find him now!' Albrecht cried.

'Now, now, Albrecht,' said Dave, holding Albrecht back. 'Rules are rules. First, we dine.'

Dinner Time Rules

Section One:

THE **SHORTEST WIZARD** is in charge of the mustard and must wear the **TEA TIME HAT**

MUST BE TALL

Not to be confused with

PUT THE LID BACK ON THE KETCHUP

Senior Wizards only

APPROVED CUTLERY

FORK   KNIFE   SPOON   CURLY STRAW

Junior Wizard UNLESS

must sit on a pig

DO NOT PUT...

Only at Christmas

elbows, Knees, face or behind **ON THE TABLE**

especially on

DURING A FULL MOON

YOU MUST SIT BACKWARDS

NO TROUSERS

Oh my!

SPAGHETTI NIGHT

CHAPTER 6

As he sat down at the long dining table, Dave decided to have a quick look at the Dinner Time Rules in the book before the soup was served. It all seemed very complex.

'Shortest Wizard wears the Tea Time Hat!' yelled Arnold over the ketchup. 'Someone pass Dave the Pretty All Right the mustard.'

'Oh my!' said Dave. 'Wait, what do you mean short?'

Dave didn't have much time to think about his new hat because just at that moment someone had decided to make a flashy entrance.

Oh my! Now this is a very special hat.

FROG SAUCE

P S

MUSTARD

Dave stared. 'That tiger is a tad bigger than I expected but he's probably just a really big pussy cat right?'

Barry growled, pounced on Arnold and took a big bite out of his hat.

'Oh,' said Dave.

'I say, Terrence!' said Arnold from under Barry. 'I don't think that's quite fair!'

Terrence sniggered. 'I don't think it's against The Rules now, is it Arnie? Reginald, what would you say?'

Terrence's Assistant Fox peered over his spectacles and said, 'No Sir, Guild Rules do not mention tigers, only lions, sharks and hedgehogs.'

Dave looked over at Albrecht and noticed that he had gone very pale.

Through gritted teeth he said to Dave, 'I do not know how I can just sit here like a Dummkopf and watch that life-ruining wizard bully people! I should go and show him the skills I learnt during my time as a super ninja! I have hooves of steel…'

'No, Albrecht! We must bide our time. Staying in disguise might help us find the animals without getting into a huge fight.'

'But huge fights are mein best thing!'

Dave put a hand on Albrecht's arm and noticed he was shaking. 'Do some of the breathing exercises Mildred taught you. Go to your happy place.'

As Dave was trying to get Albrecht to do a little meditation, he noticed one wizard who obviously hadn't gone to their happy place. While all the others cowered into their badger soup this one hopped up onto the table.

Terrence had gone a little purple in the face. 'Oh is that what you think Wizard Brian!? Well, don't you know that the junior wizard is required to shut their stupid mouth when a more awesome wizard is talking?'

'Rule 1,887 does state, and I quote, that "all junior wizards must respect their elders, even if they are idiots",' added Reginald.

'Exactly!' said Terrence. 'I am the eldest and therefore the most senior wizard. You have to do what I say! Now, Barry needs his dinner and, of course, all rule breaking must be punished. Barry, EAT THAT WIZARD!'

'Erm,' said Arnold from the floor, 'really a punishment should be decided by the Council and it's more like litter picking or no dessert?'

'That kitty isn't really going to eat the wizard is he?' Dave whispered to Albrecht.

As Terrence dissolved into a fit of fairly evil giggles, Barry leapt across the table and swallowed Wizard Brian whole.

'Really!?' said Dave.

CHAPTER 7

'That is not a nice kitty!' said Dave.

'I agree that these are not good table manners,' said Albrecht. 'Tigers and wizards, mein Dave, they're both as bad as each other, but that Terrence is the worst!'

'We've got to do something!' said Dave. 'There's got to be spell or something in the book.'

Potion to tame a huge, Angry Beast

Troll on the loose ? Giants on a rampage ? Auntie in a bad mood ? Just combine these common household ingredients in a Couldron and simmer for 15 mins to make a potion that will make the drinker disappear! Also good for Cold sores.

Half a Newt

Goblin Horn

Assorted Eyeballs

Dust of a Fallen Star

Cat Claws

Ketchup

'Perfect!' said Dave. 'I'm not sure that we have quite the right ingredients here so I'll have to improvise.'

I think it might need more salt

Once Dave had finished his potion, he waved the bowl in the direction of Barry. 'Hey, Mr Tiger! I've got the perfect second course. I call it… Really Very Nice Wizard-Flavoured Soup!'

'Oh, how did you know? My favourite!' said Barry who promptly ate the soup, bowl and all.

Barry ran out of the room, probably looking for a toilet.

'Well, that wasn't what I expected but I suppose it kind of worked,' said Dave.

Terrence was not pleased.

WHEN I AM THE MOST POWERFUL WIZARD EVER, EVER, EVER YOU'LL ALL RESPECT ME!

'Why would anyone respect him?' said Albrecht. 'Not only is that Dummkopf a bully, he is so wound up it's like he is wearing an Unterhose six sizes too tight.'

All the other wizards tittered with laughter.

'You're all MORONS!' said Terrence. 'As soon as I find Barry you're all going to be tiger meat!'

He overturned his soup bowl, gave poor sticky Brian a kick and stormed out the room. With a sigh, Reginald followed.

See you later tight pants.

Yum, parfait

CHAPTER 8

'Are you OK?' said Dave to a slightly dazed and somewhat wet Wizard Brian.

'I was just eaten by a tiger but apart from that I'm just fine,' said Brian, taking a seat at the table and dabbing at his beard with a napkin.

'You're very brave and sticky for a junior wizard,' said Albrecht.

'I'm only the junior wizard because The Rules say so! I am working on becoming the best wizard ever, don't you know.'

'Kleiner Brian,' said Albrecht. 'I like you. You remind me of a young, dashing, me with your ambitions and gooey beard. Now, can you tell us more about Terrence the Terrible. What's his deal?'

'Oh, Terrence! We all hate him. He stole Ian the Illusionist's pencil case, he pantsed the Amazing Arnold last Tuesday, not to mention letting his tiger eat me just now! No one will stand up to him because of the stupid rules.'

'We want to stand up to him!' said Dave. 'In fact, we heard a rumour that he'd kidnapped a load of innocent animals which we want to rescue! Do you know where he might be keeping them?'

'He's certainty up to some super sneaky stuff,' said Brian thoughtfully. 'Terrence is always hidden away in his private rooms, working on something but he won't tell us what. I've never been up there.'

'Mein Brian, is there anyone who knows how to get to that Hintern-kopf Terrence's rooms?' said Albrecht.

'Mabel, do you know the way up there?' asked Brian.

Dave and Albrecht looked around to see where exactly Mabel might be until some irritated coughing from underneath Brian caught their attention.

Hey there.

'Oh hello!' said Dave 'You must be the junior wizard's chair. I've read about you in The Rule Book.'

Mabel sighed. 'People are always forgetting I'm here. It's because I'm a chair. Or is it because I'm a pig? Anyway, I don't like talking about Terrence! If he finds out I've been talking about him he'll lock me away with the other animals again! I much prefer being a chair.'

'Oh no, we'd never tell on you!' said Dave.
'Albrecht is no snitch!' added Albrecht.

'Yes, thanks, Albrecht,' said Dave. 'Anyway, we're here to save all the talking animals!'

Mabel perked up. 'Save us? Leave the Guild? I've read about spas that have muds baths in Terrence's beauty magazines and I'd love to go one day!'

So, Mabel tried to explain where Terrence had kept her when she was first captured. 'I'm not entirely sure where the rooms are. I only got out of there because one day Terrence had a tantrum and kicked me out of the window.

Luckily, I landed in the Guild's duck pond, swam back to the building and another wizard plonked me in the dining hall thinking I must be the junior wizard's chair. I've been here ever since eating leftovers and putting up with Brian's bony bottom!'

'Hey!' said Brian.

'Terrence's rooms must be up very high, in the attics right above the duck pond. When he wasn't threatening to make me into a bacon sandwich he'd mutter about needing more talking animals for his "evil plan" so he could become the most powerful and popular wizard ever. He also bought a lot of shampoo.'

'Terrence shouldn't be able to push people around, kick them out of windows and feed them to mean kitties!' said Dave. 'And his table manners are just awful. We have to DO SOMETHING! It's just so mean.'

The other wizards lost interest in their badger soup and started to pay attention to Dave's rant.

'But Dave the Pretty All Right, he's the Senior Wizard,' said Clive. 'We can't disobey him, it's against The Rules! There's nothing more important than rules, obviously.'

This speech had started to get away from Dave a little. 'Well, err, The Rules are . . . wrong! We need to unite! If we all stick together and work as a team we can defeat that bully Terrence. I know we can do it! Wizards, ARE YOU WITH ME!?'

Well this
is
awkward...

CHAPTER 9

'Err, no,' said Arnold, 'we're not with you because it's 10.17 p.m. and Rule 52,406 says we have to be in bed by half past.'

Dave was disappointed. He thought the speech had been very inspiring. 'But Brian! We could really change things!'

'I tried standing up to him Dave and I got eaten by a tiger,' said Brian. 'And I suppose they are the rules even if I don't like them. I'll never be an excellent wizard if I disobey and get kicked out of the Guild.'

'Don't worry, mein Dave,' said Albrecht, 'we've all had our disappointing revolutions.

'Anyway, I can defeat Terrence singled hoofed!'

'No, Albrecht! We work best when we work together!' said Dave. 'For example, I remembered to pack our pyjamas.'

Dave and Albrecht were allocated bedrooms because in the Guild of Wizard bedtime straight after dinner is compulsory.

'I really wanted to share a room with you Albrecht,' said Dave. 'Instead, I have to share with the strange guy who keeps pulling coins from behind people's ears.'

'It does not matter for we shall not sleep!' hissed Albrecht. 'If you insist on us working together we shall meet in the corridor at midnight to search for the animals! It shall be very sneaky, secret and kind of like a slumber party.'

So Dave and Albrecht passed the time in their rooms until midnight. Neither of them enjoyed it much.

CHAPTER 10

At 11.30 p.m. Albrecht decided that patience was for Dummköpfe so he snuck out of his room. As Albrecht peered into the dark corridor he caught sight of something odd.

'What is this small hoppity hop?' thought Albrecht. 'Its fluffy white hintern suggests to me that it is a clue! I shall pursue.'

Albrecht trotted off into the shadows after it. He rounded a corner and came face-to-face with a little fuzzy bunny rabbit.

Oh, hello Mr Wizard. You must help me! I am but a poor rabbit who The Terrible Terrence made talk. I nibbled my way out of my cage and escaped, but who will save all the others I left behind? Terrence will be back soon!

'Albrecht shall help them of course!' Albrecht struck his most heroic pose. 'I made a promise!' But what about Dave? There was no time to go back for him and this could be his only chance to save the animals. Albrecht would have to go alone.

'I shall have this wrapped up by breakfast and Dave shall be so impressed. Now, you must lead me to Terrence's rooms, schnell! And I alone will rescue my friends . . .'

Albrecht never got the chance to finish because from behind him in the gloomy corridor he heard a voice say, 'Hello, Albrecht, old friend.'

And then, before Albrecht could catch his breath, everything went dark.

CHAPTER 11

At exactly midnight Dave snuck out of his
room to meet Albrecht. He was distracted by
Wizard Brian who was quietly tiptoeing towards
the toilet. But not just any toilet, the cobweb-
covered, barely used ladies toilet! In a place
where girls are not allowed, that's very odd.
Dave had to investigate.

Dave silently shuffled into the ladies loo ...
Wait a second! Wizard Brian is ... A GIRL!

Dave gave a little hiccup of surprise and stumbled over. Brian spun round.

'You! Dave the Pretty All Right! If you ever tell anyone what you've seen I'll … I'll… saw you in half or pull something really nasty out of my hat or turn you into a frog or something! I'm a serious wizard you know.'

'Brian! I don't care if you're a girl, a boy or a three-headed hippo! It doesn't matter and of course I won't tell anyone. I'm very good at secrets. Look! I'm not even really a wizard.'

Dave took off his own beard and gave his chin a good scratch.

'Oh wow, you're a real-life dragon?!' said Brian. 'Dragons are shorter than I expected.'

'Yes, and you're more of a girl than I expected, but surprises are fun, aren't they?'

'Is it true about all the riddles and gold and village eating?'

'Some dragons are into that stuff. I'm more of an adventurer now because of my friend Albrecht who's my mentor, spirit guide, trusty steed and also a goat.'

'That explains a lot. I thought he smelled goaty,' said Brian.

Dave nodded. 'Brian, can I ask, why do you want to be a wizard so badly that you have to pretend to be a boy and wear an itchy beard?'

Brian began to explain. 'Well, I used to be called Belinda, but to be honest I prefer Brian now.'

Brian used to work in the kitchen of the nearest castle where her mother was the cook. Brian was in charge of breakfast.

She used to do bacon baps, cereal, a continental option, but mainly porridge.

One day a travelling
wizard came to
their village.

TADAA!

WOW.

He did amazing things like making
a ball disappear or pulling a rat
out of a hat.

A what?
Sometimes
we use rats
when on
a budget.

That was when Brian knew she wanted to be a wizard but her mother had other ideas.

GIRLS CAN'T BE WIZARDS! You should try and find a nice boy to marry instead.

Brian didn't want to marry anyone so she came up with a plan.

BAH?

stay still.

Snip!

Perfect.

'So I set off for the Guild of Wizards that very night. I would learn all the spells, make all the

potions and become the best wizard ever! Even
if I had to live a lie, it would be worth it. Things
aren't going to plan though. I've been trying
my best to learn from the books but the other
wizards are all very jealous and won't share their
tricks. Terrence is the worst! He's a bully, always
trying to trip me up in the halls and getting his
fox to file law suits against me. And the rules!
There's so many here that they get in the way of
learning anything. I'm sick of sitting on Mabel at
dinner... but there's something else.'

Brian looked down at her feet, ashamed.

'What is it?' said Dave. 'Don't worry, you can
tell me. I'm very open-minded. My best friend is
a pungent goat after all.'

'I'm... I'm not really a very good wizard.
There's only one trick I can do and it's not
proper magic like card tricks or making coins
appear. It's kind of weird and icky.'

'I can't even do the flower trick right, so any
magic will impress me,' said Dave.

Blushing, Brian reached out and touched the
sink and with a 'SPLURGE!' the sink was no
more.

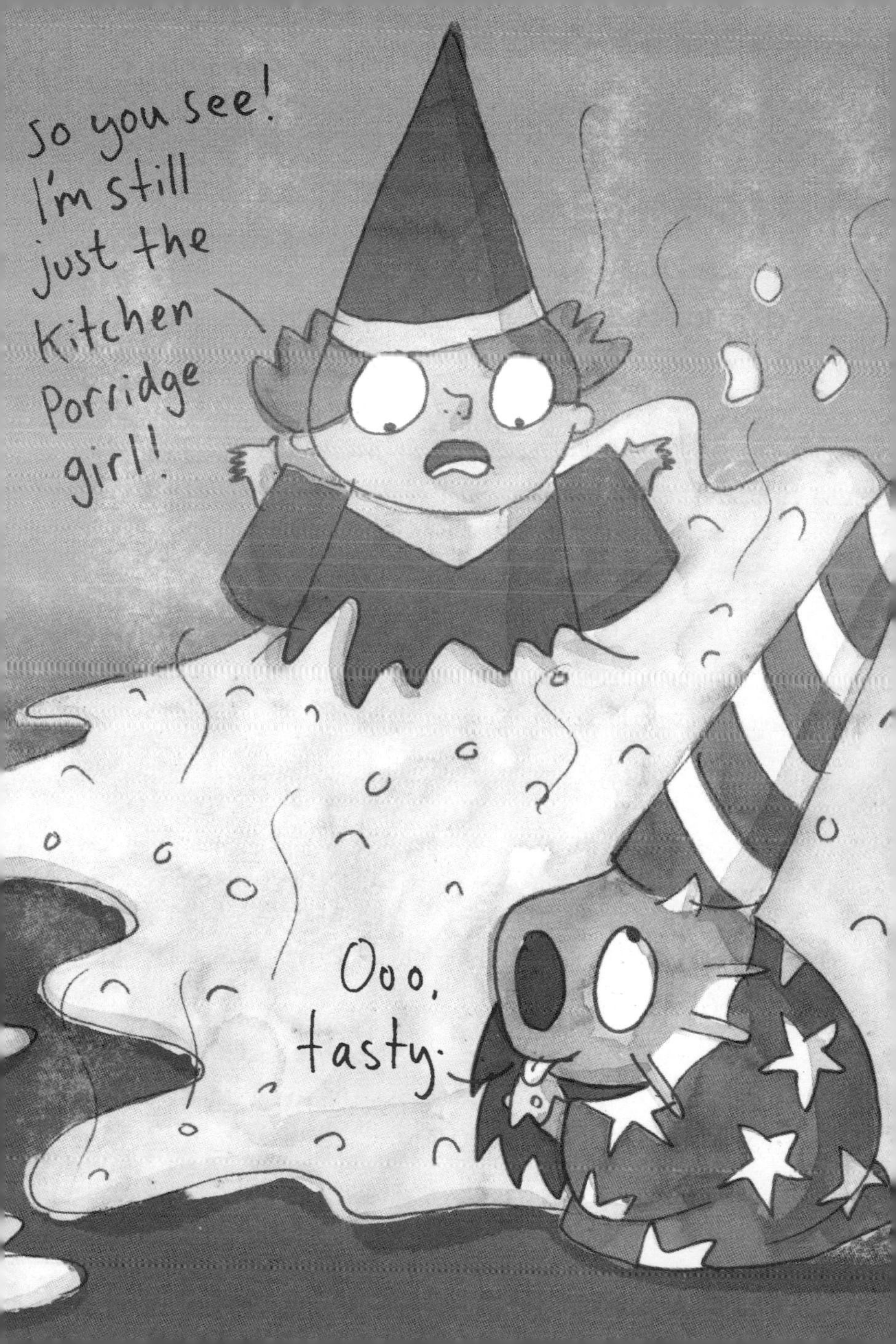
So you see! I'm still just the Kitchen Porridge girl!
Ooo, tasty.

'Porridge!' thought Dave. 'Well that's…
different.'

But then Dave was not exactly a standard
wizard, so he was not about to judge Brian.

'Don't worry, Brian,' said Dave. 'You shouldn't
be ashamed. In fact, it's pretty great! Porridge
is my favourite breakfast. I'll try and help you
become the best wizard ever. Maybe in return
you could help me too?'

Dave explained about the talking animals, Terrence the Terrible, and Albrecht. Wait a minute, where was Albrecht?!'

We have to go and find him! If I leave him alone for too long he challenges people to duels or tries to tell them about his autobiography!

CHAPTER 12

'Stop right there gentlemen!'

Brian and Dave froze.

'Oh brilliant, that's Terrence's lawyer,' said Brian.

'At least it's not Barry again, he's much worse,' said Dave.

'You wizards are out of bed after lights out which is a flagrant violation of Rule 783. Show them Andrew!'

Reginald's assistant, who was already armed with the Rule Book, opened it and presented a page to Dave and Albrecht.

Being out of bed after lights out is punishable by expulsion from the Guild and no breakfast!

'Don't think breakfast will be a problem for us,' Dave gave Brian a nudge.

'Breakfast isn't the thing I'm worried about, DAVE!' said Brian.

'OK, OK. Hang on.'

Dave got out his copy of *Wizarding for Beginners* and flicked through until he found the rules section.

'Aha!' said Dave. 'Look, there an exception to that rule!

* unless it's for a really good reason.

'We're trying to rescue some animal friends of mine!' said Dave. 'That's a *really* good reason.'

'I see,' said Reginald, narrowing his eyes. 'Andrew! Go to subclause 236!'

✳✳ Really good reasons only include needing the loo, midnight snacks, and fire alarms.

'Darn!' said Brian. 'We should have said we needed the loo.'

'Wait! I've read the chapter on rules three times, Mr Fox. There's a sub-subclause about this!' Dave went to a page right at the back of the book.

✳✳ All wizard disputes can be settled by the outcome of the Guild's traditional sport.

'So be it!' said Reginald. 'Andrew, wake up the guild, it's time to play Magic Ball!'

CHAPTER 13

'I don't understand why the Guild's solution to being out of bed in the middle of the night is to get everyone else out of bed to play Magic Ball,' said Brian.

'It does sound like nonsense,' said Dave. 'Where's Albrecht when you need him? He would know what Magic Ball was, for sure. He knows everything.'

'Have a look in your book,' said Brian.

MAGICBALL

3-Man Magic Ball Squad

A game played with mallets where the ball shape shifts when struck. A skilled wizard can control what the ball will become. This is a key tactic. Played in teams of 3. First to score 2 wins.

unchanged Ball

fig1. Mallet

←Goal→

serving circle

teamA

←TeamB

TeamA

TeamB

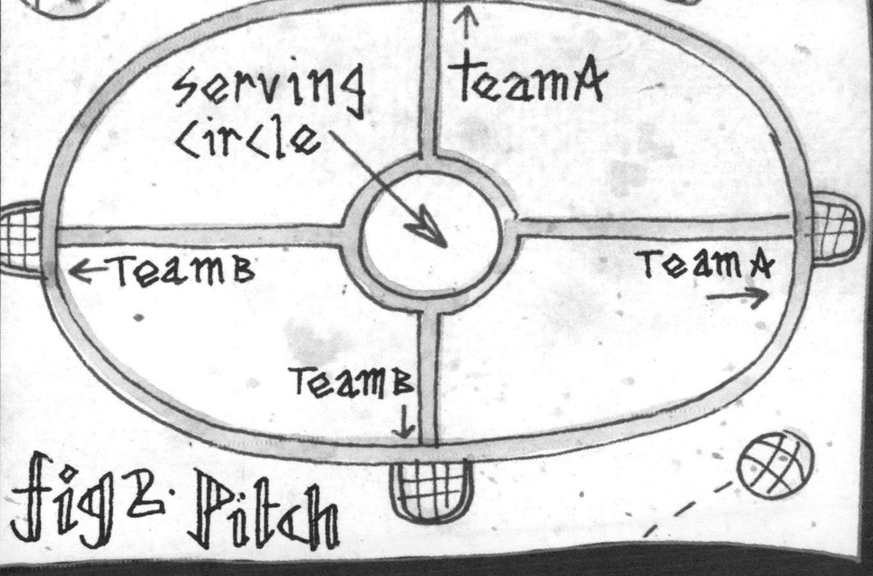

fig2. Pitch

'It actually sounds rather fun,' said Dave. 'Albrecht would love the uniforms and competitiveness. Why don't you like it?'

Brian looked at her shoes. 'I can only turn the ball into one thing.'

'Oh yes, of course,' said Dave.

Brian looked across the pitch and saw Clive give the ball a warm-up whack and turn it into a lobster. Arnold returned it and with a poof it became a lawn mower.

'Dave, the other team is made up of the Guild's best players. Clive is surprisingly gifted with a mallet. How can we win this? I can only make porridge and you can't even do magic.'

'Apart from the flowers trick!'

'I'm not sure flowers will help. Plus, we're one player short.'

Just at that moment, something came jogging across the field.

Hello chaps, I heard you're short a player. I'm the Librarian. I was a prime Magic Ball player in my day and I'll take any opportunity to stick it to Reginald!

The Librarian began some warm-up stretches.

'Thanks, very kind sir, but, um, are you wearing any clothes under all that beard?' said Dave.

'The Rules don't say anything about clothes! Plus, I have only just got out of bed,' said the Librarian as he bent over to touch his toes.

The Librarian squinted at Dave. 'You remind me of someone, Dave the Pretty All Right . . .'

'Maybe you know my Aunt Maud! She's a Librarian too,' said Dave.

'Oh yes, old Maudie!' said the Librarian. 'I met her at a conference way back.'

'I won't ask why a wizard has a dragon for an aunty,' he said with a wink.

Before Dave could really think about that or ask which way round to hold his mallet, the first whistle blew and the game began. They made a strong start.

My Serve! Hedgehog!

POOF!

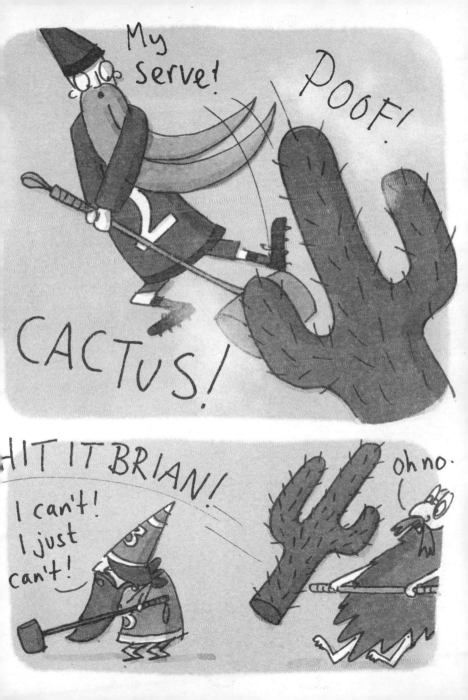

POOF!

Airplane!

I'm out of the game chaps.

GOAL!

1-1

We need to win this point Brian but it's ok. do your best. I don't mind whatever happens.

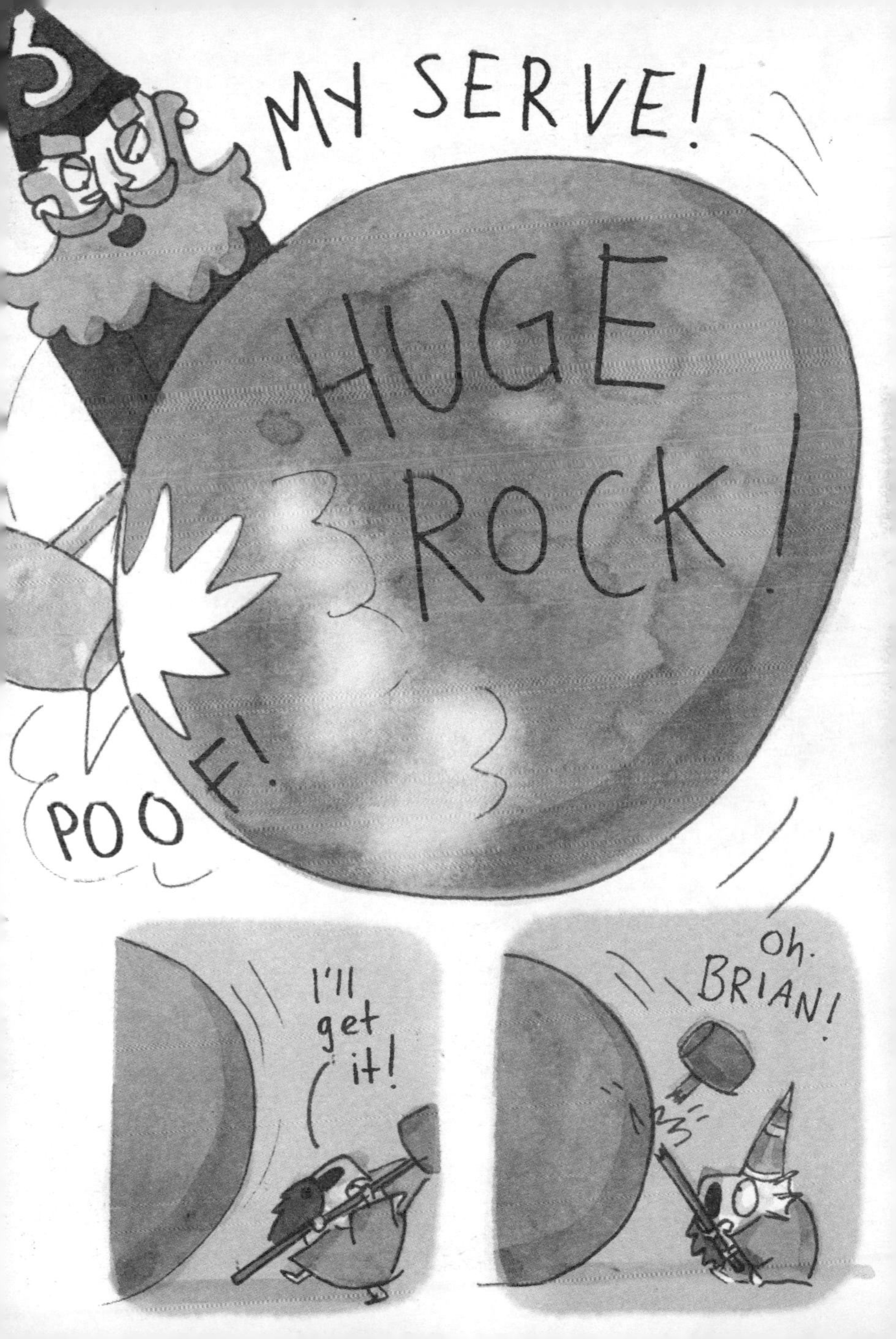
MY SERVE!
HUGE ROCK!
POOF!
I'll get it!
Oh. BRIAN!

WINNERS

'Good game chaps!' said the librarian. 'Now Reginald, you have to let these two young wizards go. We won fair and square and it's The Rules after all.'

From under his coating of porridge, Reginald bristled. 'Well I never… I can't really… this is a…. FINE! You win! Oh my good gracious, I've never been let down by The Rules before! I didn't become a lawyer to just let people… ANDREW! Get me a latte!'

At this, Reginald flounced off the pitch, his assistant trailing behind him.

'I can't believe it!' said Brian. 'I've never even hit the ball before in a Magic Ball match! What a team we are, Dave! Dave?'

Dave was frowning off towards the edge of the pitch.

'Something's not right Brian. It's not like Albrecht to miss out on a victory celebration, especially when there's a chance to wave a trophy around. I've got a really bad feeling.'

The Librarian put a hand on Dave's shoulder. 'Can I lend a hand, Dave the Pretty All Right? Anything to help a Magic Ball teammate.'

Dave told him everything about the kidnapped animals, Albrecht, and Terrence.

'I know where that Terence hides out. I have to deliver library fines to his rooms all the time! He keeps taking out books about hairdressing and bringing them back VERY late. Hang on, I'll draw you a map.'

CHAPTER 14

Brian and Dave burst into Terrence's rooms. But Terrence was nowhere to be seen. And neither was Albrecht.

Dave was distraught. 'If Albrecht's not here, where could he be? Usually he's very easy to find because of all the shouting and people running the other way! This can't be good.'

All the animals started talking at once.

'WAIT!' Brian stepped into the middle of the room. 'One at a time, please! Frog guy with the crown, where is Terrence and have you seen Albrecht?'

Gilbert hopped forward. 'Terrence was here earlier, going on about how he had finally found an animal with a coat glossy enough to complete his spell so that he can become the most powerful and popular wizard ever.'

'I think I know what Terrence was talking about.' Brian grabbed the book out of Dave's hand. 'I've read about this before while I was kind of studying but mainly looking for a way to make my hair less frizzy. Look at this!'

He built the first Guild of Wizards, bringing unity to all wizard-kind.

Despite this, he still wasn't satisfied.

This could be glossier.

So he set out to use all his power to make a shampoo like no other.

But things didn't go to plan.

The Guild was destroyed and he saw the error of his ways.

My beautiful hair! I cannot be trusted with this power!

So the Wizard vowed to never use his power again.

He put all his power into one object that became known as...

THE MAGIC WAND!

The Guild of Wizards was rebuilt and The Wand was hidden deep underneath so no one would make the same mistake again. Only one deemed worthy by the glossiness of their hair can stand in the secret spot, say the magic words and claim The Wand as their own.

Dave had gone a very pale shade of green. 'Oh my, now I understand. Terrence wants to be the "Best and Most Popular Wizard Ever" and he thinks The Wand will make him that. He needs someone really, REALLY glossy to get it. But who could be so glossy that they... oh no'

Oh no, oh my, oh dear, (ALBRECHT!

CHAPTER 15

While all this had been happening, Albrecht was being carried around in a sack with an awful lot of hair products. Naturally, it wasn't the first time he'd been in a sack. He once had to disguise himself as potatoes to sneak aboard a ship bound for the tropics. For some reason though, he had a really bad feeling about this, and it wasn't because of the shampoo bottle sticking into his Hintern.

Dave! If only Dave were here. He could tell Dave all his sack stories and fun facts, they'd escape in some daring way he'd devise, and maybe Dave would even do something useful. Sacks just aren't any fun without Dave. Also, he was so squished up he starting to lose the feeling in his hooves.

'For my dear friends, I must prevail!' Albrecht cried, and gave the sack an experimental kick.

Albrecht was tipped out of the sack onto a damp cellar floor. He looked up and saw exactly what he didn't want to see.

Albrecht spotted the rabbit from the corridor. 'Kleiner hare! That wizard is most evil. We must run before it is too late!'

The rabbit hopped down. 'You don't understand goaty man. It was all a very clever plan from wonderful Terrence to trap you. I'm Miriam, Terrence's first and best talking animal, occasional toupee and very best friend!'

'We're not friends!' said Terrence. 'We're work colleagues at best. Actually, I'm more like your boss.'

Miriam looked hurt. 'But what about all those years we spent together when I was your only friend?'

'Miriam! SHUT UP!' Terrence looked at Albrecht. 'She knows nothing. I'm very popular and fun to be around.'

'I do not care that a Dummkopf like you has no friends! I, on the other hand, had many close friends and acquaintances until you stole them. What are you doing with those animals? I demand you free them immediately!'

Terrence gave him a particularly smug grin. 'Oh Albrecht, you glossy fool! I don't want those dull and dishevelled animals. It's YOU who I need.'

Terrence began to stare wistfully into the middle distance.

'Mein Gott, I feel a flashback coming,' said Albrecht.

Terrence shushed him and began his story. 'For years I've been trying to claim The Wand so I could be the BEST WIZARD EVER EVER EVER. Finally, I would be respected and, most of all, POPULAR! Only one thing stands in my way…

'...The Magic Mirror!

'To get The Wand a worthy wizard must stand before the Mirror in the Secret Spot and say the Magic Words. If the Mirror judges you to have the finest hair, to be the "The Glossiest of Them All", it will give you The Wand.

The only problem is the Mirror is super judgy and kind of a jerk. It was really mean about me!

But then I had the most ingenious of ideas. If I was not glossy enough then I'd find someone who was. What could be glossier than an animal with luscious fur or shiny scales? I was already the very best at the talking spell. There's no animal I can't make talk, even the very stupid ones! I would get the glossy animals to say the Magic Words for me and then I'd claim The Wand for myself!

It's obviously the best of plans, but finding the perfect animal has proved tricky.

Too stripy.

Too feathered.

Trying too hard.

So boring.

A total mess.

Too ginger.

Hey!

What are you thinking?!

Too creepy.

Just silly.

Do you think you're in a boy band?!

Are you cleaning that with your mouth!? Ew! No.

Hate the
fringe.

Hair! Not
fins.

'I even tried putting Miriam in a wig.
'Every time we made the
dangerous journey to the Secret
Spot my animal was rejected.
'Then one day, when I was
passing a simple farmhouse,
I saw THE ONE!

Just no.

The Glossiest Of Them All

bah?

But of course, Albrecht, you escaped before I could take you to the Secret Spot. For many years I searched for you, but you were always one step ahead.'

'I am a fast-paced dynamic go-getter,' mused Albrecht.

'Shut up, this is my flashback!' said Terrence. 'It was your foolishness, your stupid friendship, that finally gave you away!

'The only question was how would I trap such a trixy goat as you? I'd learnt that if I tried to capture you again you'd only evade me. So, I would have to make you come to the Guild of your own free will. What better way than to lure you here to save your animal friends! You could never resist playing the big clever hero, Albrecht. Now The Wand is in sight and all I need is for you to shut up, come with me and do as you're told.'

If you think I'm going to come quietly Wizard you're a bigger Dummkopf than I thought.

Stay still while I add some of this for extra gloss.

SUPER SHINE SRRAY

CHAPTER 16

Dave was not coping well with the idea that Albrecht had been kidnapped.

'What am I supposed to do without Albrecht? I've never adventured alone! How am I going to defeat an evil wizard who's obsessed with power and hairstyles and rescue my trusty steed all at the same time?! We don't even know where this "Secret Spot" Terrence is heading for is.' Dave went back to breathing into the paper bag.

'I'm going to help,' said Brian. 'There's no way I'm letting that bully Terrence get The Wand. He'll make this place even worse and make even more rules! They'll all be Terrence Rules like "everyone has to compliment Terrence's beard" or "everyone must wear a T-shirt with Terrence's face on it" or "everyone has to let Barry eat them". NO WAY. We've done a pretty good job of adventuring together so far. I never thought I'd win a Magic Ball match.'

Dave looked up from the bag. 'Yes, I suppose we have made a pretty good team, and I have already learnt a lot of things about adventuring from Albrecht. If he's taught me anything, we should probably strike an adventurous pose, stride into the face of danger, and think about whether we can use this in our autobiographies or not.'

Dave stood up, puffed himself up, strode forward, and then slipped straight over onto his bum.

'Owie,' said Dave.

Brian looked down at him. 'I don't want to bring the mood down or anything, but I'm not sure I want to write an autobiography... hang on, what was that you slipped on, Dave?'

Dave looked at the floor where he noticed a puddle of something sticky. A trail of it went all the way to the door. He sniffed it.

'It smells like forest fruits and glossy shine. It's shampoo! Albrecht must have left us a trail to follow. He's so clever.'

Secret Spot
I refuse to breathe in! I will not be a part of your evil plan and I do not like what that rabbit has done with my hair!

If Barry can fit through that hole you can too.

CHAPTER 17

Deep in the cellars of the Guild of Wizards, Terrence had reached the passageway to the Secret Spot. Albrecht was not making things easy for him though. 'I will not go down there you bearded Rotzlöffel!'

Sometimes, thought Albrecht wistfully, all you needed was a little help from your friends. Dave would do the wunderbar job of slowing the wizard down. He'd talk to Terrence about all his

Dummkopf feelings for hours until Terrence was all sniffley, crying. Maybe Albrecht could do this too! He'd seen Dave have lots of chitchat with people who he thought were über-boring. He would ask questions and pretend to be interested. Just like Dave.

Albrecht cleared his throat and shouted back to Terrence, 'So, er, is not the weather so nice Herr Wizard, and why do you want to be the MOST POWERFUL AND POPULAR WIZARD EVER, anyway? Only foolish people chase power.' Albrecht stopped himself because he thought Dave probably wouldn't start by calling him an idiot.

It was quiet for a moment and then he heard Terrence say, 'Oh well! Really? The animals almost never want to know about how brilliant I am! I knew you were different, goat. I'm just trying to get the respect I deserve. I have always been a gifted wizard. I always obeyed The Rules and did things by the book, but even as a boy no one recognized my brilliance.

'But I don't like these memories because it makes me feel weird inside! I was totally right anyway and those idiots just couldn't see it. I needed someone who really understood me, who could recognize my genius and do as they're told. That's when I invented the talking spell and created Miriam.'

Stay still bunny! Soon I'll have someone to talk to.

'And we've been super best friends ever since!' shouted Miriam.

'Shut up, Miriam!' said Terrence. 'But one rabbit wasn't enough. When I've got The Wand and all its power everyone will finally see how awesome I am!'

Albrecht rolled his eyes. Getting Terrence to talk was working but he'd never heard such rubbish in his life. He couldn't do this listening anymore; he had to tell this wizard exactly what he thought.

'Any goat knows you get respect by earning it, not by being a DUMMKOPF!'

'WHAT DID YOU CALL ME!? Right, I'm not being patient with you any more goat! Barry, you headbutt him through this hole even if it ruins his hairstyle. We're going to the Magic Mirror!'

CELLARS

← WINE CELLAR
CHEESE STORE →
← SECRET PASSAGE
SWIMMING POOL →

CHAPTER 18

Dave and Brian had followed the shampoo trail as fast as they could, so they weren't far behind.

'Somehow I get the feeling this might be the way in,' said Brian.

'Wizards aren't very good at secrets, are they?' said Dave.

'Rule 3,546 says that everything must be properly labelled.'

'Of course. Just in case they haven't signposted the whole journey, I'm just going to check the dungeon map. There's one in the back of the book.'

'Well, that wasn't encouraging,' said Dave.
'Actually, it's rather terrifying. What even is a
"Super-Sized Killer Worm"?!'

Dave put his head through the hole. It was
incredibly dark and smelled old, musty, and
damp, rather like he imagined a Super-Sized
Killer Worm must smell.

Brian popped her head in alongside Dave. 'It's
only a worm. They don't even have legs. Shall we
go through together?'

Dave and Brian made their way down through
the passageway as it wound deeper and deeper
below the Guild of Wizards.

Dave kicked something over in the dark and
it made a clonking sound all the way down the
passage.

'WAH! MONSTER!?' said Brian.

'No no, it's just me, don't worry!' Dave reached
down and picked something up. 'Hair spray!
They must have come this way.'

SOLID SHINE
Looks like someone took care of the skeleton army.
CLONK!

Dave stumbled a little in his surprise.
'WAH! MONSTER!' said Brian.

'No, don't worry,' said Dave, 'just me again.'
'NO! Look, Dave, really!' said Brian. 'A
MONSTER!'

I AM UNHAPPY ABOUT THINGS!

CHAPTER 19

There had been many times since Albrecht went missing that Dave had wished he'd been there, but if there was any time that you needed a slightly mad goat adventurer with no regard for his own safety by your side, it was when there was a huge monster running towards you.

Albrecht wasn't here though. This time Dave would just have to be his own Albrecht.

'I shall defeat this monster with my incredible magic and then tell everyone about it! Just like Albrecht,' said Dave.

'See,' said Dave, 'everyone loves flowers.'

The monster gave the flowers a big sniff. 'How did you know? My name is Pansy and tulips are almost kind of like pansies, so this is sooo special! I'm sorry I was a little cranky just then. That mean man who's always coming down here just came through with some animals. He made his tiger fight me and now I'm all owie.'

Pansy showed Dave a scratch on her massive paw. 'People are often so mean to me, just because I'm a huge, terrifying monster. It really hurts my feelings.'

Sometimes I just feel so lonely.

There, there.

Dave patted Pansy on a huge claw. 'Well, you're not alone now,' said Dave. 'How did you come to be down here?'

Pansy brightened up a bit. 'A long time ago, I owed a wizard with really nice hair a favour, so I said I'd guard the place where his snazzy wand is kept. I don't think I'm doing a good job though. Every time that Terrence comes down here he sets his big kitty on me.'

'If it's not rude to ask,' said Dave, 'why are you scared of a tiger? You're a huge monster.'

'There's this magic mirror in the next cave that keeps saying hurtful things about my hair even when I brush it. It's so bad for my self-esteem! I just don't have the self-confidence to defend myself. They always get past me. I feel like the worst monster ever. You are the first person to be nice to me in centuries, Mr little green wizard! I wish I could leave these caves but I can't because I made a promise and monsters never break their promises.'

'You can stick with us so you won't be lonely,' said Brian. 'Frankly, it's just exciting to find another girl in the Guild of Wizards, even if you do have massive teeth and are covered in fur.'

'But I don't want to go anywhere near that kitty or it will scratch me again.'

Dave thought about this. 'Oh well, he's probably quite upset too. That man you mentioned, Terrence, stole the tiger from his home and put a spell on him to make him talk. I imagine he must miss his family. I think he needs a friend; someone to give him a compliment or a bubble bath or a nice big hug to make him feel better.'

The monster looked shocked. 'So the kitty has an owie too? Owie feelings! When I see that kitty I'm going to hug him so hard it'll squeeze all the owie out.'

Pansy grabbed Dave and Brian by the hand and pulled them away. The three of them set off along the passage towards a dim light up ahead.

Miriam, is THAT what you're doing with your fur? At least brush it!

CHAPTER 20

At the Secret Spot things didn't look good for
Albrecht.

Terrence wasn't having a great time either.

'Oh. My. Godness. Terrence!' the Magic Mirror rolled its eyes. 'That look is sooo last year. When will you do something new with your beard? I hope no one sees us together. So embarrassing.'

'Quiet Mirror!' said Terrence. 'If I wasn't totally sure of my own awesomeness that could really hurt my feelings. Anyway, I've got someone so glossy to show you that you'll be left speechless.'

'The only thing that leaves me speechless is Miriam's *terrible* split ends.'

'But I've really been making an effort with my shampooing!' Miriam hopped off looking hurt.

Terrence ignored this and went over to where Albrecht was strung up.

'Now Albrecht, stand in front of that mirror, say the Magic Words and get me The Wand, NOW!'

Albrecht was trying to look dignified, which is tricky for a goat who's tied upside down by their hooves. 'I will never let you have The Wand. My glossiness should only be used for good!'

'Oh, but Albrecht I think you will,' said

Terrence. 'You see that concoction bubbling away below you, that is my very own "Shut Your Face" potion. It's made in the opposite way to the talking spell so whoever it touches will lose the power of speech. If you don't do as you're told I'll dip you in it, and you know what that means, Albrecht?'

'This is an outrage!' said Albrecht. 'I am one of the Kingdom's finest public speakers!'

'It means you'd have no more adventures, you wouldn't tell any more stories, you'd never tell anyone else what to do, and you wouldn't be able to talk to your stupid friends. You'll just go "BAH!" for the rest of your life!'

'Mein Gott, you do not mean…'

'Yes, that's right Albrecht, you'd be…'

'Suspense is just so passé!' interrupted the Mirror. 'Could this BE any more boring. Get on with it.'

'Calm down, I'm getting there!' said Terrence. 'Albrecht, you would be… A NORMAL GOAT!'

Albrecht's eyes widened. 'I will not be bullied by you Terrence. You might think The Wand will make you über-powerful and so popular, but you will always be the same wizard bully.'

I shall use my last words to call you a DUMMKOPF!

Dave had been watching everything from behind a rock. If Albrecht couldn't talk, he would never able to give Dave advice again. They would never have a chat, Albrecht would never be able to tell his stories. Dave couldn't let this happen.

Before Brian could catch hold of him, Dave leapt out of his hiding place and sprinted over to Albrecht.

'That takes care of your silly little green friend,' said Terrence. 'Don't eat him Barry, this is so handy!'

'Albrecht, if you won't save your own voice, maybe you'll save your friend's. Get me The Wand or I'll dunk this Dave in the potion and he'll never speak another word!'

That was too much for Albrecht. It was one thing to sacrifice himself in a noble and supercool way, but not Dave. He'd never hear Dave ask anyone clever questions again, say nice things to people or tell Albrecht how super amazing he is. He could not let that happen.

'You are a worthy foe, Herr Wizard,' said Albrecht. 'Cut me down and I shall do as you say.'

Albrecht stepped up to the Mirror and said the Magic Words "Mirror, mirror on the wall, who is the glossiest of them all?" I mean, obviously it is me, but I thought I should ask.'

'NOOOOO,' shouted Dave.

CHAPTER 21

'So shiny, so healthy, so GLOSSY!' shrieked the
Mirror. 'Do you condition? Who cuts your hair?
Have you thought about modelling? Yes, take
The Wand. Take it!'

'I cut my own hair, and ja, I have thought about modelling. I was once a well-respected catalogue hoof model,' said Albrecht.

'Enough!' yelled Terrence, snatching The Wand away from Albrecht. 'This is MY moment!'

Brian was worried. She had stayed exactly where she was, hidden behind the rocks. With Dave and Albrecht captured and Terrence with The Wand, she was going to have to do something. How she was going to save the day with only an emotionally fragile monster and the ability to make porridge on her side, she wasn't entirely sure. Hang on; maybe an emotional monster might be just the thing . . .

Brian looked over at the monster who had been hiding her eyes since she caught a glimpse of Terrence and got scared. 'Pansy, look! That nice kitty is over there. Now's your chance to hug him all better.'

Pansy looked up, caught sight of Barry and began pounding across the cave. 'I'm coming mean kitty! Pansy will hug all your owie away!'

While Terrence was trying to free his tiger from the overly friendly clutches of Pansy, Brian saw her moment. She crept out from behind her rock and tiptoed over to help Albrecht untie Dave.

'Hello Brian,' whispered Albrecht. 'I am using my most secret voice because I see you are sneaking. During my time as a ninja I used to sneak all…'

'Albrecht, I've missed your stories but now we really need to get that wand off Terrence,' said Dave. 'Thanks for helping, Brian, but hurry!'

'There is still time for manners Dave!' said Albrecht. 'Brian, I must introduce you to my new friend. Compliment Mirror, meet Brian; Brian meet Mirror.'

The Mirror, who until now had been gazing adoringly at Albrecht, caught sight of Brian. 'Oh, what do we have here? That beard just looks so *fake*. I know a bad wig when I see one. BAD HAIR ALERT! BAD HAIR ALERT!' rang out through the cave.

Before any of them could shush the Mirror, it became obvious that Brian had been spotted.

There was only one thing, Dave thought, that could stand up to The Wand.

'Brian! You must use the porridge. Use the POWER OF PORRIDGE!'

'I can't! It's *porridge* Dave,' said Brian, 'not some incredible, powerful spell. I'm just not that sort of wizard!'

'You've done some amazing things while we've been adventuring and some of them even

SPLOT

involved porridge,' said Dave. 'I believe in you
and I believe in breakfast. DO IT!'

'Enough of this emotional rubbish,' said
Terrence. 'First new rule I'm going to make is
NO MORE BRIANS!'

Terrence raised his wand to blast Brian but
she reacted just in time.

ZZAP!

Soon a fight was underway. A fight quite unlike anything the Guild of Wizards had seen before.

SPLOT

ZAP

That's loud.

Sounds like it's coming from the cellars.

Shall we investigate?

After breakfast.

PIGEON FLAKES

But there was one thing Brian hadn't counted on—Miriam!

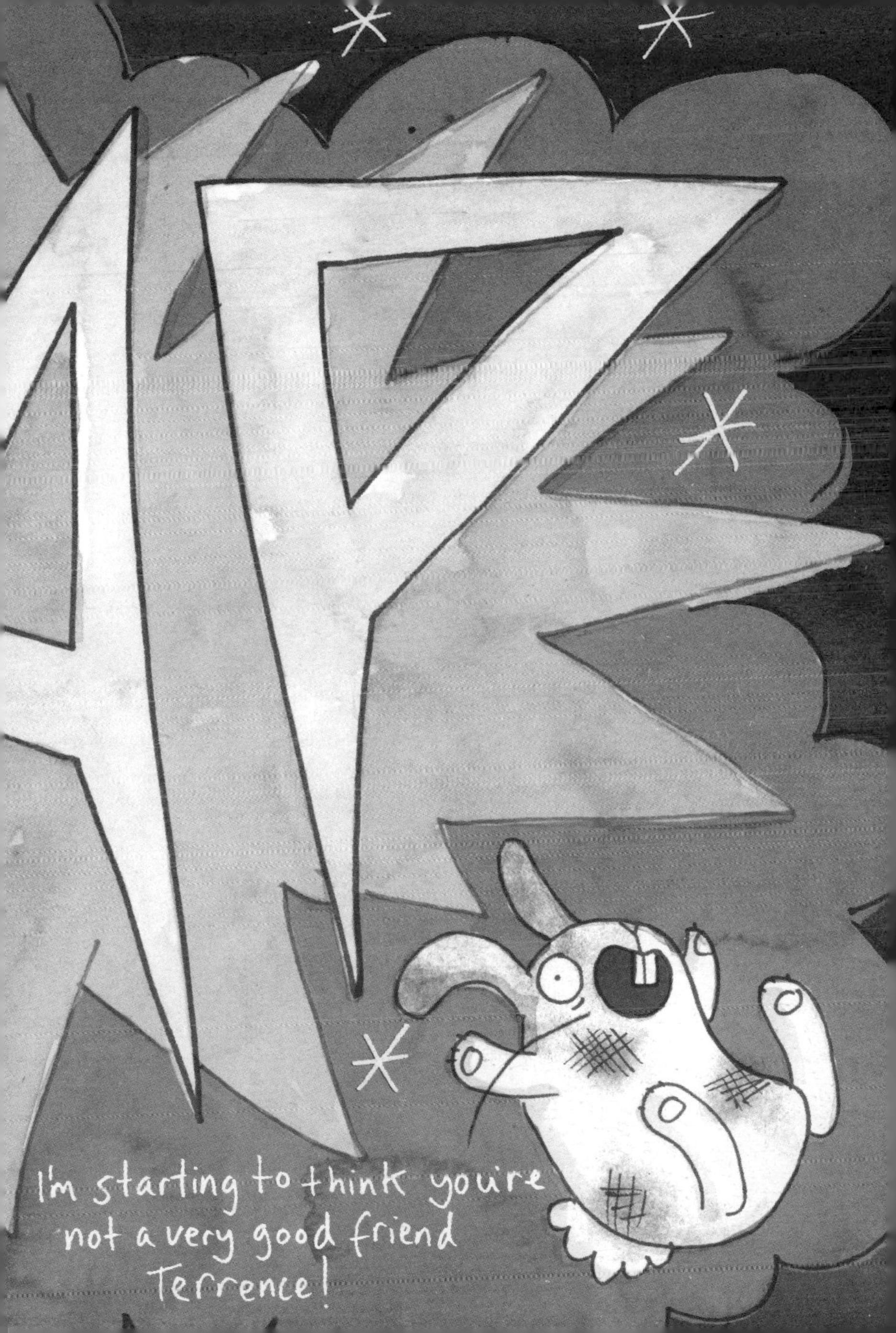
I'm starting to think you're not a very good friend Terrence!

CHAPTER 22

'Brian! Brian was hit!' Dave shouted across the cave. 'BRIAN! Are you alive?!'

Brian was surprised to find that she was alive. Something wasn't right though. She felt around and discovered she still had all her arms, legs, fingers and even her nose. Then Brian looked in the Mirror.

It took a while for Albrecht to stop the Mirror from screaming.

'WHAT!' said Terrence. 'This wand should have blown that pathetic Brian and her breakfast foods into a million pieces. What sort of rubbish "all powerful" wand is this?!' Terrence chucked the wand to the floor and began to stamp on it.

'Is that what it does?' said Dave. 'This amazing, legendary wand that we've been fussing over all day gives you BAD HAIR?'

'Even I am underwhelmed and I really didn't want the irresponsible wizard idiot to have unrivalled power,' said Albrecht.

'What were you expecting? The Wizard Fabilo was obsessed with perfect hair. For him, what power could be more dangerous?' said Brian. 'Do you think I can comb this out?'

Dave was hit with a sudden realization.

'Brian, I don't want to alarm you, but I think your beard has melted.'

Terrence looked up.

'HA HA! How Hilarious! Brian's a GIRL!

'That violates the very first rule of the Guild of Wizards!'

Terrence looked towards the other wizards. 'See! Brian can't be the winner of this fight because she's not even a real wizard. Brother wizards, we must banish Brian immediately! Girls can't be trusted with magic. She'll make everything all girly.'

Brian was surprised to find she didn't feel afraid that she'd been found out. Actually, it was quite a relief and for the first time in ages her face wasn't itchy. What she was starting to feel was angry. She'd just done some pretty amazing, if fairly porridgey, magic, better than any of these wizards. How dare Terrence tell her she wasn't a real wizard? What does making 'everything girly' even mean?! Brian was about to porridge the lot of them when the Librarian stepped forward.

'Do you know what, Terrence? I've had enough of your bullying and I've had enough of these rules! Do you know the reason I don't wear clothes is that Rule 88,765 says the Librarian must be nude during working hours?! That's ridiculous!'

'Then why are you nude during your time off?' said Clive.

'That's a personal preference. I say enough of these rules and no more lies! It's time to tell the truth.'

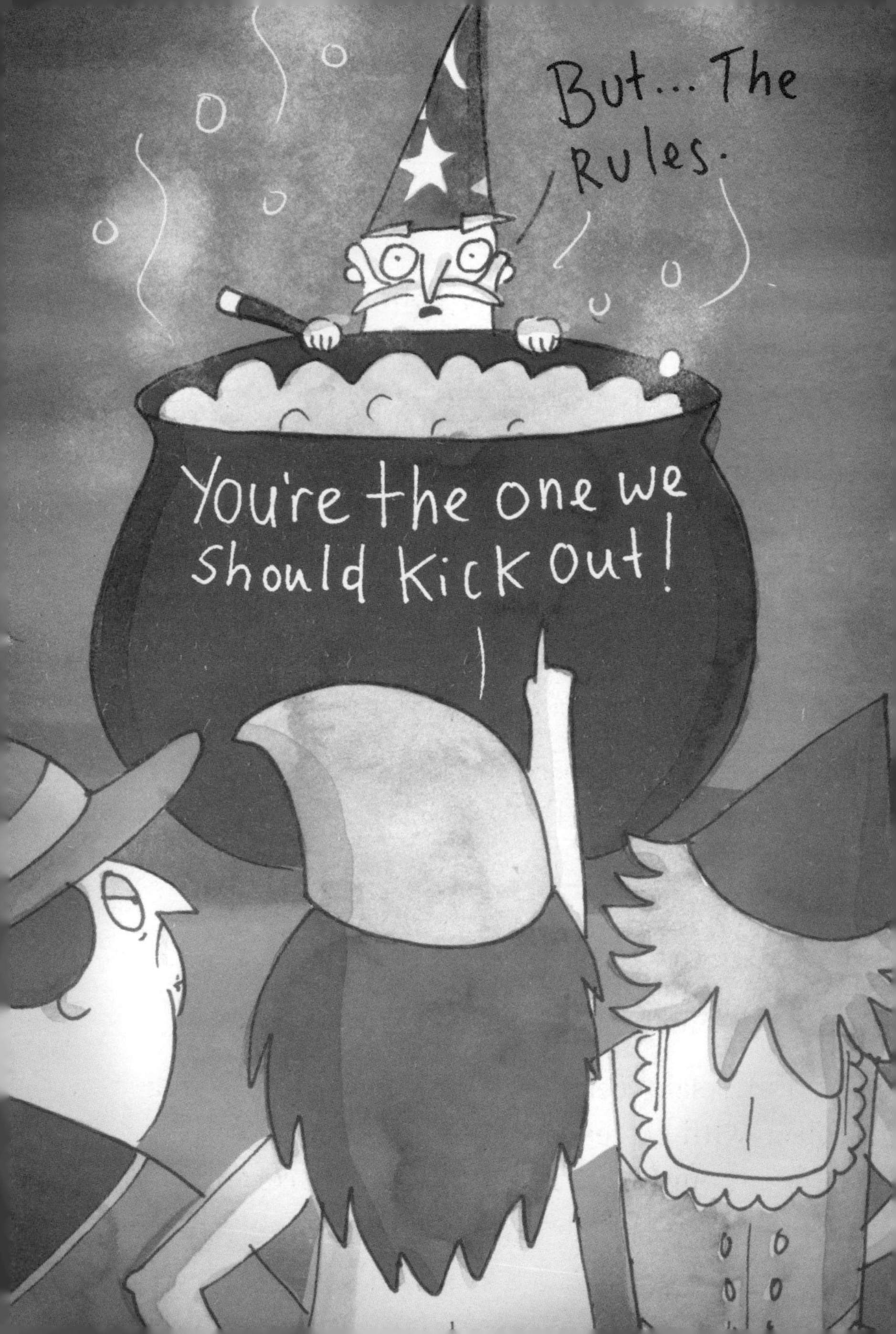
But... The Rules.
You're the one we should kick out!

'All I ever wanted was to properly organize magic books,' said the Librarian, 'and I don't see any reason why I shouldn't be able to do that, beard or no beard!'

'I just wanted to play Magic Ball professionally,' said Clive.

'And I just really like the hats!' said Arnold.

Terrence seemed to be having some trouble processing what had just happened.

BUT THIS BREAKS ALL THE RULES!

'Fine!' said Terrence. 'I don't want to be in a place with no respect for The Rules, anyway. First though, I'm going to have my revenge . . .'

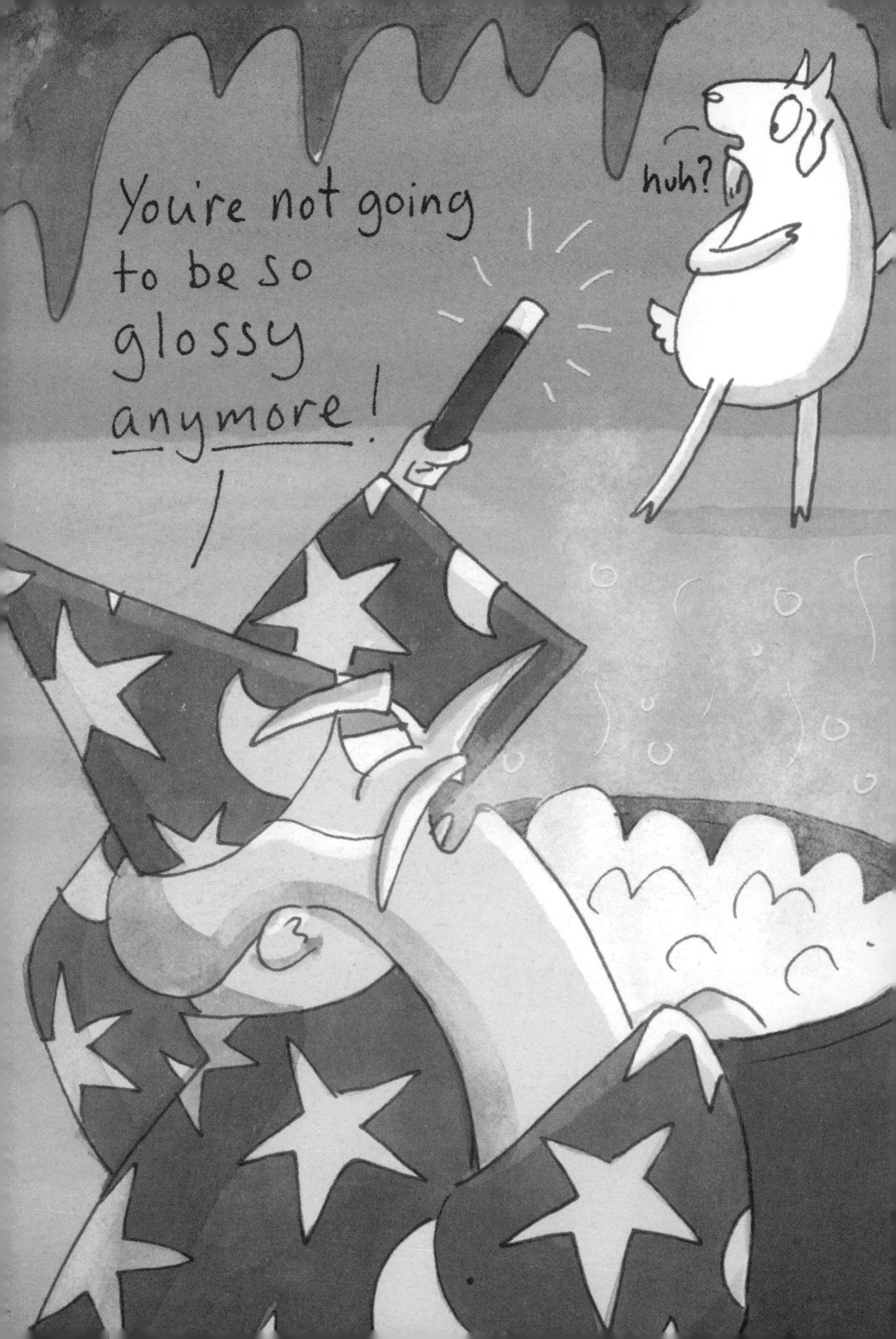
huh?
You're not going to be so glossy anymore!

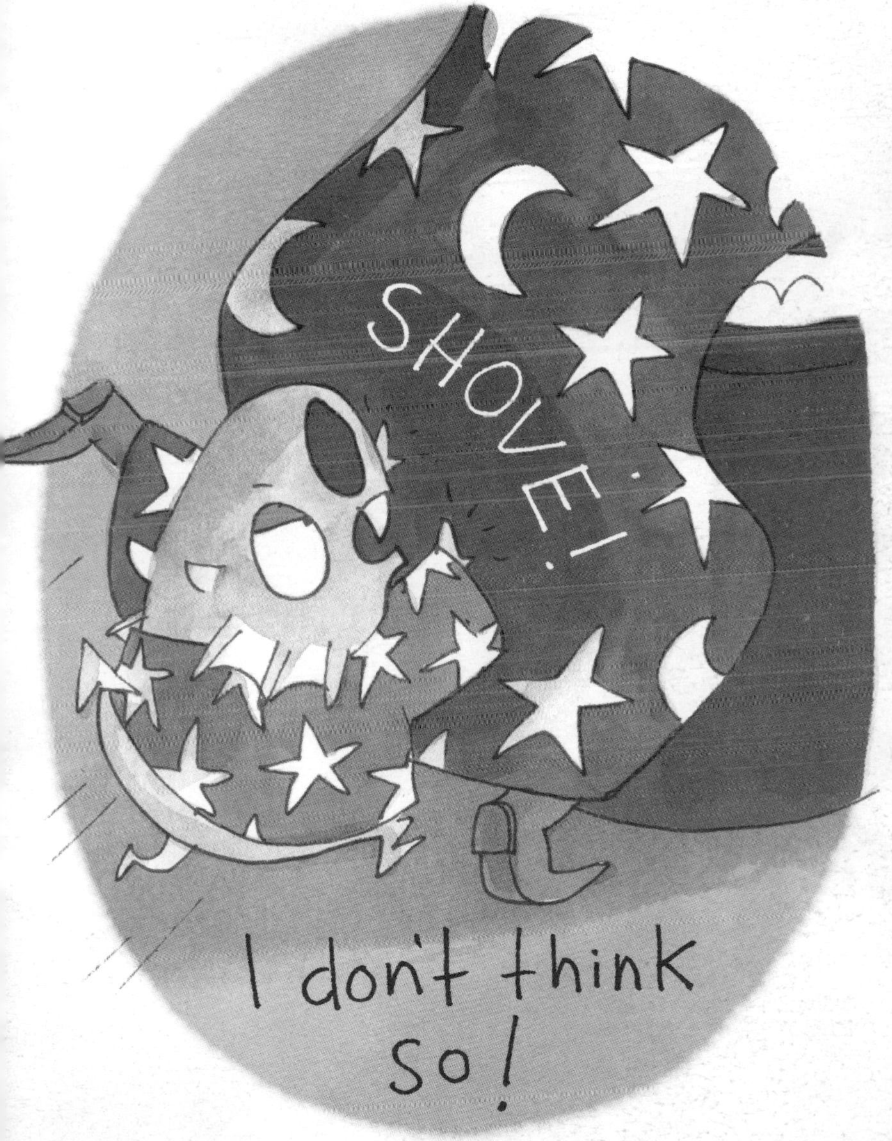
SHOVE!
I don't think so!

Don't mess
with Albrecht.

I can't believe you threw ANOTHER book at a villian Dave. We must do some more herotraining when we're back.
It seemed like a good idea at the time.
EVERYONE WELCOME

CHAPTER 23

Outside the Guild of Wizards things were quite different. Wizards were throwing off their beards, celebrating, and no one was worried about being late for dinner.

'I think I'm going to write a new version of *Wizarding for Beginners*,' said Brian. 'There'll be lots of suggestions, handy hints and tips, and a whole chapter on porridge. Look, I've already made a start.'

'I'm still working on the structure,' said Brian.

'Amazing! That's a book I want to read. You'll have to send me a copy for my book club when you're done,' said Dave.

Brian looked a little crestfallen. 'Are you sure you don't want to stay? We could start a book club here?'

'That is very kind Brian, but it is time for the next adventure!' said Albrecht. 'I must reunite with my family and find some way to communicate with them. This adventure has taught me that no goat is an island and friends and family are über-important. Also, I am really super glossy and that is a marvel that the world must see.'

'That's as sentimental as Albrecht gets,' smiled Dave. 'I'm going to meet them too! I hope I make a good impression. Can I keep this hat? I think it's very smart.'

'Why not?' said Brian.

'Über-magischer Brian,' said Albrecht. 'What did you do with The Wand? Power to destroy such glossiness cannot be allowed!'

'Don't worry,' said Brian. 'I've given it to someone who I'm sure will take very good care of it.'

Dum de dum...

Dave and Albrecht said goodbye to Brian. They promised to send many letters, exchange porridge recipes and haircare tips, then set off to find Albrecht's family.

'What will you do for the journey, mein Dave?' said Albrecht.

'Oh well, the Librarian gave me a little light reading. That should keep me busy for a bit.'

BEARD STYLE

Robes Robes Robes
FOR ALL YOUR ROBE NEEDS

CARING FOR YOUR RABBIT

Some time and several books later, Albrecht was reunited with his family. Even though they no longer shared a language, it didn't seem to matter one bit.

AND THEY ALL LIVED HAPPILY EVER AFTER:

After realizing The Rules aren't always right, Reginald quit working for Terrence and now defends talking animals who have been wrongly accused of crimes.

How could this animal be guilty your Honour?

SENIOR

Andrew has been promoted to Senior Assistant.

Brian published her book (which was very well reviewed in the Castletown Chronicle).

THE BRIAN GUIDE TO WIZARDING

FORWARD BY ALBRECHT

She was declared Senior Wizard by popular
demand and started her own book club.

As it turns out, Barry did miss home and needed
a hug. Pansy helped him find his way back to the
jungle. Pansy's self-esteem is now very high.

The Amazing
Arnold's love of
squirrel parfait
led her to open a
restaurant. Now
she's Castletown's
best-known celebrity
chef.

Then you dip the squirrel in the parfait...

Magical Mark rather
liked her fake beard
and to this day still
wears it in the bath.

Clive is now a
professional Magic
Ball player. She was
recently sold to
Goblin United for
the record sum of
$12 million.

Having lost his voice, Terrence took a job as a mime artist and now does children's parties.

He still doesn't think he gets enough respect, but Miriam thinks it's the best thing that ever happened to him.

After recent events, the Librarian decided it was time to catch up with some old friends.

That's my nephew!

Dave and Albrecht are currently taking some time out before the next adventure comes along. Dave has kept up the magic but Albrecht still finds it suspicious. On the first Sunday of the month Brian joins them for breakfast.

Porridge anyone?

PIGEON FLAKES

Finally, Albrecht did publish his autobiography. Dave isn't sure how accurate it is.

And so, I battle with my life long nemesis, the Dummkopf wizard.

At last I defeated him with nothing but my good looks.

Once again I was a hero and Dave was very impressed.

Albrecht's German for Dummköpfe

aufwachen – wake up

dumme – stupid

Dummkopf – fool, blockhead (singular)

Dummköpfe – fools, blockheads (plural)

Fräulein – Miss, young lady

Guten Tag – Good day

Herr – Mr

Ich kann sprechen – I can speak

ja – yes (pronounced yah)

kleiner Drache – little dragon

kleine Suppenwerfer – small soup thrower

Können Sie mich verstehen? – Can you understand me?

magisch – magical

mein – my

mein Dorfesser – my village eater

mein Hintern – my bottom

mein Gott! Ich kann sprechen! – My God! I can talk!

mein Dave – my Dave

mein kleiner grüner (friend) – my little green (friend)

Rotzlöffel – snot-spoon

Sauerkraut – pickled cabbage

schnell – quickly

über – outstanding, utmost, extremely

Unterhose – underpants

wunderbar - wonderful

Elys is an author and illustrator currently living and working in Cambridge. She works predominantly with ink, newfangled digital witchcraft, and coloured pencils, of which she is the proud owner of 178 but can never seem to find a sharpener. When not doing pictures and making things up, Elys enjoys growing cacti, collecting pocket watches, and eating excessive amounts of fondant fancies.

Knighthood for Beginners is Elys Dolan's first young fiction book and was shortlisted for the Branford Boase Award; her hilarious picture books have been shortlisted for *The Roald Dahl Funny Prize, Waterstones Children's Book Prize,* and nominated for the *Kate Greenaway Medal.*

KNIGHTHOOD
for
BEGINNERS

'Full of splendid silliness' The Guardian

FROM THE
MOST BONKERS MIND OF
ELYS DOLAN

Dave dreams of being a brave, knightly knight—saving princesses, riding a majestic steed, and protecting the kingdom from all evil-doers. And when he finds a very special book, *Knighthood for Beginners*, his quest to become a knight begins!

Accompanied by his trusty steed, Albrecht, he duels with the strongest and bravest knights in the land. But his toughest test comes when he has to convince the court that being rather small, distinctly green, and, frankly, A DRAGON, is no barrier to knighthood.

Prologue

There was once a dragon. A dragon called Dave. He lived high in the mountains surrounded by the bones of those who had dared to trespass near the Dragons' Caves. He was the most terrible of dragons, with scales, and teeth, and horns, and feet …

. . . no, wait. Hang on a minute. I don't mean *that* kind of terrible. I mean he was terrible at being a dragon.

You see all dragons must abide by Dragon Lore.

A Dragon must hoard gold, gems, and all riches. He must manage it wisely and keep it tidy.

A Dragon shall riddle and riddle with vigour!

A Dragon must feast on nothing but villages.

A Dragon must knit, because of all the handicrafts, knitting is the fiercest.

To be honest no one really understands the knitting bit but they do it anyway because that's the way it's always been.

Every dragon must master the Lore by the time they come of age and take their Dragon Test. When he's passed the test a young dragon will receive his certificate and become a fully licensed dragon.

No one has ever failed.
But Dave might be the first.

He'd been up all night studying and first thing
that morning Dave's parents came in and said
they needed to have a 'serious talk'.

'Listen Dave,' said his fearsome father. 'As you know you come from a very old dragon family. We're a proud line of the most dragony of dragons. There was your grandfather who had the biggest hoard since records began, Cousin Myrtle who once ate six villages in a row, and your Uncle Kevin who knitted that lovely hat.'

'What we're trying to say,' said Dave's massive green mother, 'is that you've had the finest education, the best knitting tutor a gold hoard can buy, we've taken you to gourmet villages, and taught you our most cryptic riddles. We've tried our best to make sure you're ready, but your father and I both know you've never been the most talented dragon.'

'You spend too much time reading those books and not enough time actually being a dragon!' said Father.

Dave has a bit of a thing about books. It all started when Dave was a baby and his parents went on a village-tasting tour. They left him with his Great Aunt Maud who was a librarian. (Even dragons need librarians.)

It had a big effect on him.

And ever since then Dave feels about books like most people do about their favourite teddy. If they're not a dragon.

Dave's father bent down and looked him in the eye. 'When did you last set fire to anything?! Have you eaten a single village? And you never even finished that bobble hat…'

Mother shot Father a stern look. 'Now, Rupert, we said we were going to be calm about this. David, today is your Dragon Test and it's very important to us that you get your certificate.'

'Get out there and eat a village, son,' said Father.

'And don't forget your yarn!' said Mother.

More from Elys Dolan

STEVEN SEAGULL
ACTION HERO

STEVEN SEAGULL
ACTION HERO

ELYS DOLAN

The CLOCKWORK DRAGON